Also in this series:

 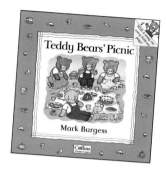

Other titles by Mark Burgess:
Teddy and Rabbit's Picnic Outing
Follow the Kite

First published in Great Britain by
HarperCollins Publishers Ltd in 2000
1 3 5 7 9 10 8 6 4 2
ISBN: 0 00 198335 0
Text and illustrations copyright © Mark Burgess 2000
The author/illustrator asserts the moral right to be
identified as the author/illustrator of the work.
A CIP catalogue record for this title is available from the British Library.

The HarperCollins website address is: www.fireandwater.com

Printed and bound in Singapore by Imago.

Teddy Time

Mark Burgess

Collins

An Imprint of HarperCollinsPublishers

'Ring-a-ding!' the alarm clock goes,
Get up teddies, put on your clothes!

What time is it?

It is 8 o'clock.

Downstairs the breakfast table is laid,
The toast is done, the tea is made.

What time is it?

It is 9 o'clock.

Then off to town the teddies run,
There is some shopping to be done.

TED'S FRUIT AND VEG Party Time FANCY DR

What time is it?

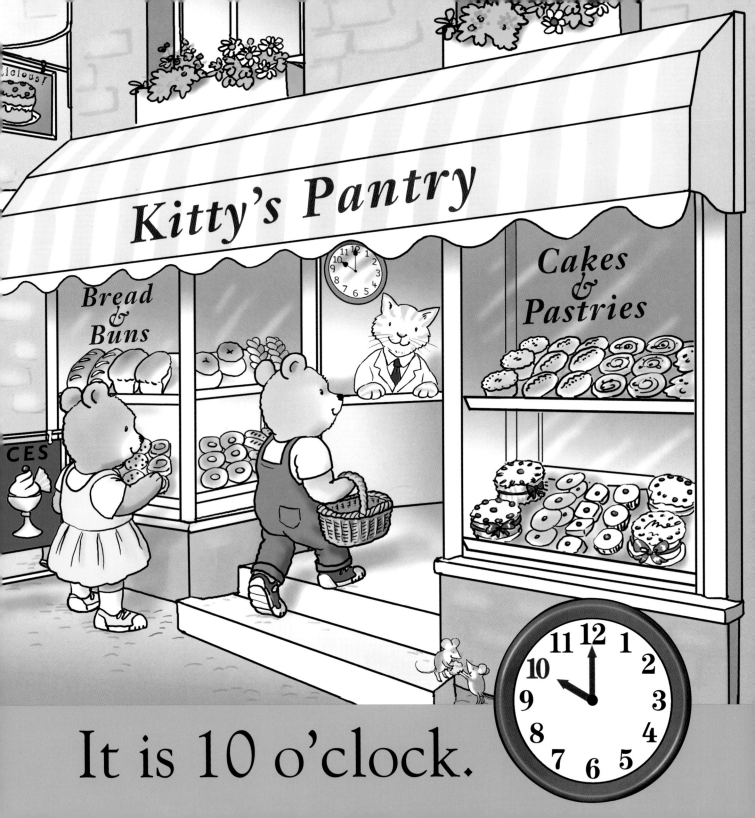

It is 10 o'clock.

They call on all their friends to say,
"Will you come to tea today?"

What time is it?

It is 11 o'clock.

Back home, as quickly as they can,
The teddies carry out their plan.

What time is it?

It is 12 o'clock.

They move the chairs, put out the plates.
Blow up balloons, arrange the cakes.

What time is it?

It is 1 o'clock.

So very busy is each teddy,
Now, at last, the bears are ready.

What time is it?

It is 2 o'clock.

The guests are here so let them in,
And now the party can begin!

What time is it?

It is 3 o'clock.

There is lots of lovely food to eat,
Four kinds of jelly – what a treat!

What time is it?

It is 4 o'clock.

Then games to play for everyone,
And dancing – come and join the fun!

What time is it?

It is 5 o'clock.

The party is over, it's time to go,
Goodbye teddies and thank you so.

What time is it?

It is 6 o'clock.

Now the bears are off to bed,
Each one of them a sleepy head,
"What fun that was," the teddies say.
"We'll do it all again some day!"

What time is it?

It is 7 o'clock.